To: Ms. Susan
With love,
Mary Ellen & Jim
2007

The Sheltering Cedar

Anne Marshall Runyon

PORTAL PRESS
WASHINGTON, D.C.

The following book is a work of fiction.

Library of Congress Control Number: 2007926202
ISBN: 978-1-933454-02-3

Portal Press
1327 Irving Street, N.E.
Washington, D.C. 20017
www.theportalpress.com

THE OUTER BANKS OF NORTH CAROLINA

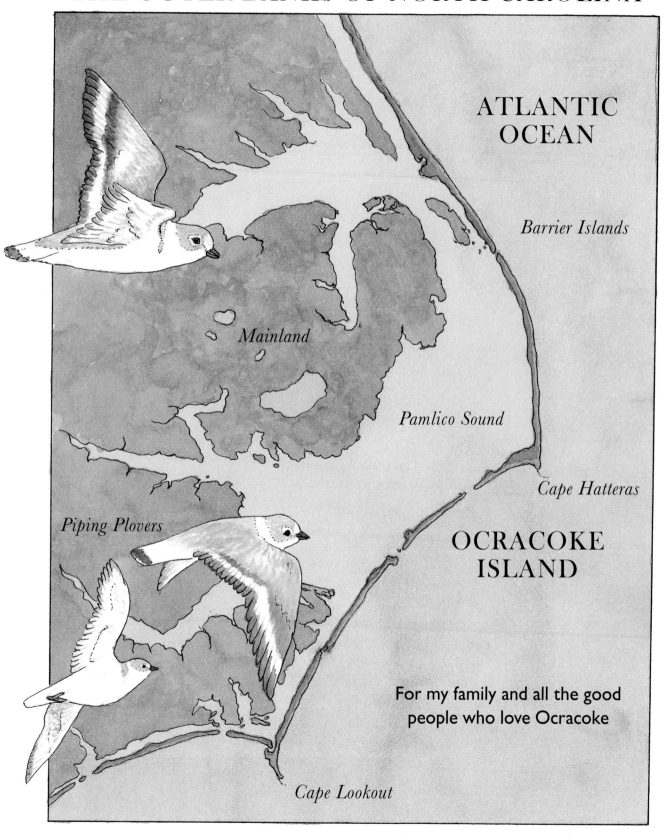

ATLANTIC
OCEAN

Barrier Islands

Mainland

Pamlico Sound

Cape Hatteras

Piping Plovers

OCRACOKE
ISLAND

For my family and all the good
people who love Ocracoke

Cape Lookout

A fierce nor'easter growls around Ocracoke Island and the old cedar tree creaks in the wind.

Black-bellied Plovers

It is the day before Christmas.
The lighthouse shines,
steady during this dark day.

PAMLICO SOUND

Harbor

Lighthouse

OCRACOKE ISLAND

Ocracoke Inlet

The Southern red cedars growing near the ocean are
bent by the winds and grow wide and low like big bushes

ATLANTIC OCEAN

Lighthouse

The cedars near the lighthouse
are sheltered and grow taller.

Cedar Tree

Hatteras Inlet

The islanders gather safe and warm
in their snug homes.

Their fishing boats shelter in the harbor.

Harsh winds howl across the beach,
blasting rain, sand, and salt spray at the cedar tree.
This weathered tree offers shelter
from the bitter storm.

Inside the sturdy tree
red birds chirp and fluff.

Four small beetles escape
the wind and rain
by crawling under
the peeling bark.

Mantid egg cases, attached to fragrant needles, ride on the wind-tossed branches of the cedar.

Two toads, cold and slow, rest among the roots,
buried in the soft, cool sand.

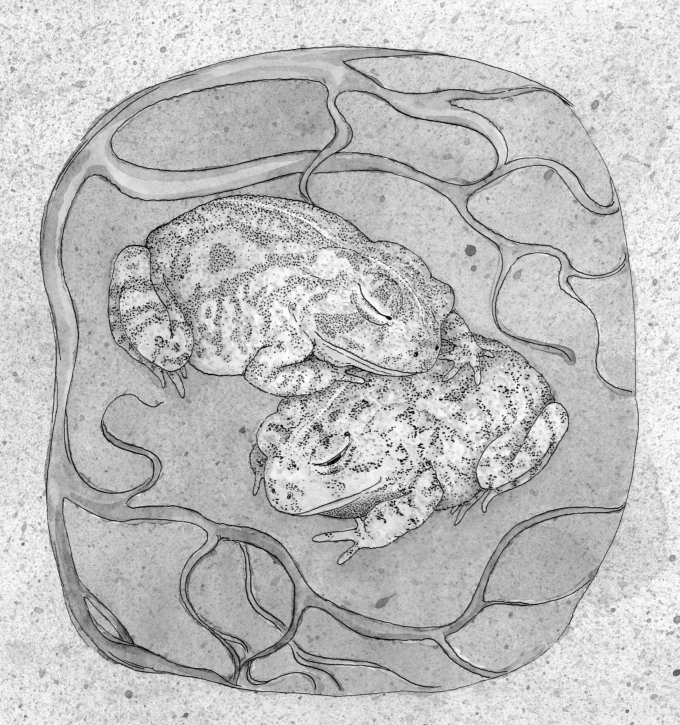

At last the fierce winds gentle and the rains
slide off across the sound.

The North star shines bright
above the cedar tree.

It is Christmas Eve on the island.

Slowly rising above the dancing ocean,
the sun warms the dunes.

One wet cedar perfumes the air.

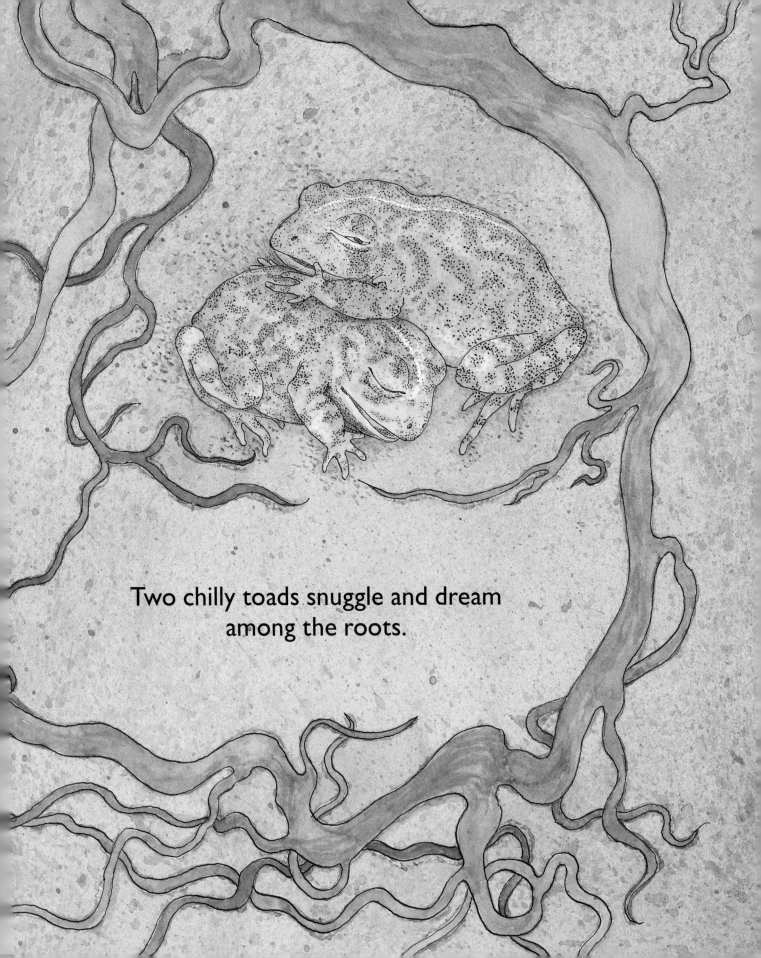

Two chilly toads snuggle and dream
among the roots.

Three mantid egg cases
glisten in the needles.

Four small beetles begin to stir,
rustling along the bark.

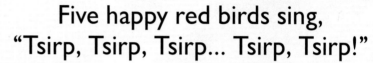

Five happy red birds sing,
"Tsirp, Tsirp, Tsirp... Tsirp, Tsirp!"

Christmas has come to the island.

Cedar Tree Facts

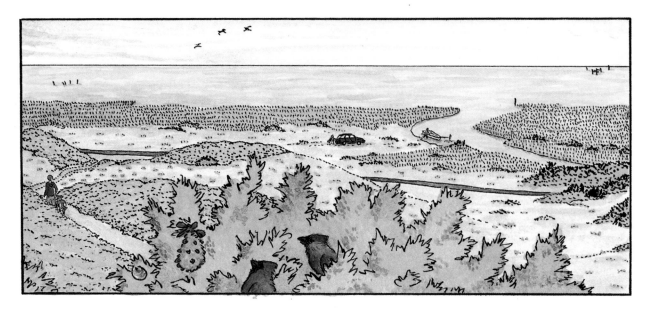

Wild winds and salt spray sweeping across the Outer Banks sculpt the Southern red cedars into wide, low-growing trees. These island cedars are evergreens like the pine, spruce, fir and Eastern red cedar trees that people often decorate at Christmastime. However, windswept Southern red cedars rarely stand tall or straight like Christmas trees.

Red cedars belong to the juniper family, and are covered with dense scale-like leaves. The new growth is prickly and bright green. Male cedars, like the one in <u>The</u> <u>Sheltering</u> <u>Cedar</u>, bear many small brown cones in the late winter. Winds carry pollen from the male cones to the green berry-like cones on nearby female cedar trees. The fertilized cones slowly ripen, turning blue with a waxy coating in the fall. Cedar waxwings and other birds eat these berry-like cones in the winter when other fruit is scarce.

male cones

female cones

female mantid and her egg case

The wild animals featured on the two previous pages are: Redbirds or Cardinals, Red-bellied Woodpecker, Fish Crows, Brown Pelicans, Yellow-rumped Warblers, Cedar Waxwings, Bottle-nosed Dolphins, White-footed Mice and a Ghost Crab.

For free paper sculptures of Cedar Tree Animals and other fun activities, visit our website at www.theportalpress.com.